WILLY
AND
HUGH

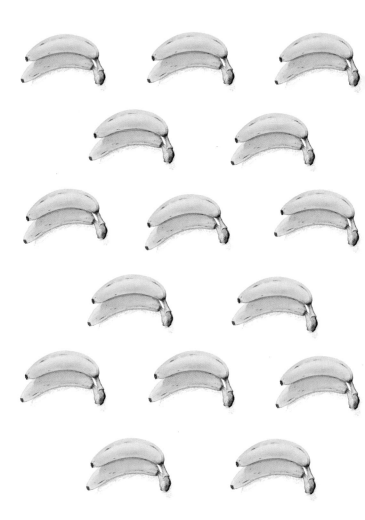

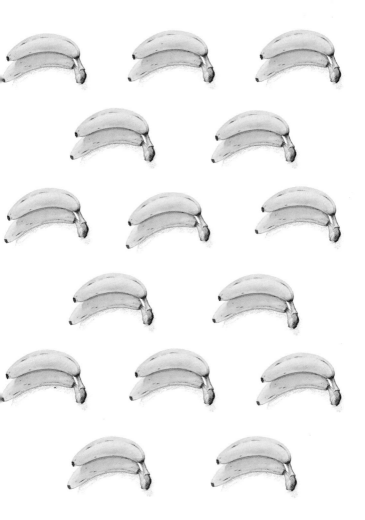

A Red Fox Book

Published by Random House Children's Books
20 Vauxhall Bridge Road, London SW1V 2SA

A division of The Random House Group Ltd
London Melbourne Sydney Auckland
Johannesburg and agencies throughout the world

3 5 7 9 10 8 6 4

First published in Great Britain 1991
by Julia MacRae

First published in Mini Treasures edition 2000
by Red Fox

Printed in Singapore.

THE RANDOM HOUSE GROUP Limited Reg. No. 954009

www.randomhouse.co.uk

ISBN 0 09 940779 5

Anthony Browne

WILLY
AND
HUGH

Mini Treasures

RED FOX

Willy was lonely.

Everyone seemed to have friends.
Everyone except Willy.

No one let him join in any games;
they all said he was useless.

One day Willy was walking in the park...   minding his own business...

and Hugh Jape
was running...

they met.

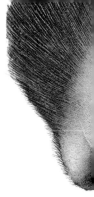

"Oh, I'm so sorry," said Hugh.
Willy was amazed. "But *I'm* sorry," he said,
"I wasn't watching where I was going."
"No, it was *my* fault," said Hugh. "I wasn't
looking where *I* was going. I'm sorry."
Hugh helped Willy to his feet.

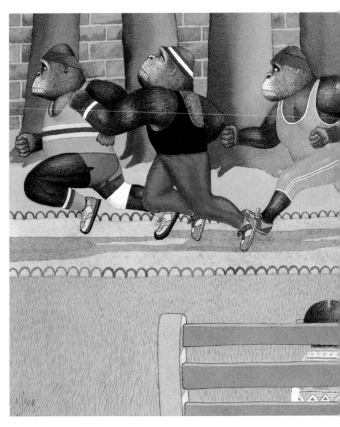

They sat down on a bench and watched
the joggers.

"Looks like they're *really* enjoying
themselves," said Hugh. Willy laughed.

Buster Nose appeared. "I've been looking for you, little wimp," he sneered.

Hugh stood up. "Can *I* be of any help?"
he asked.
Buster left. Very quickly.

So Willy and Hugh decided
to go to the zoo.

Then they went to the library,

and Willy read to Hugh.

As they were leaving the
library, Hugh stopped
suddenly...

He'd seen a
      TERRIFYING CREATURE...

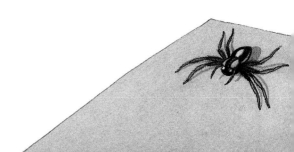

"Can *I* be of any help?" asked Willy, and he carefully moved the spider out of the way.

Willy felt quite pleased with himself.
"Shall we meet up tomorrow?" asked Hugh.
"Yes, that would be great," said Willy.

And it was.

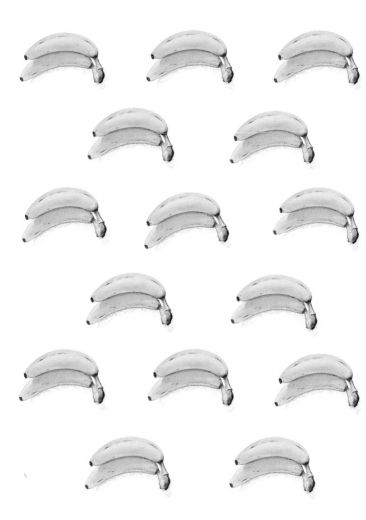

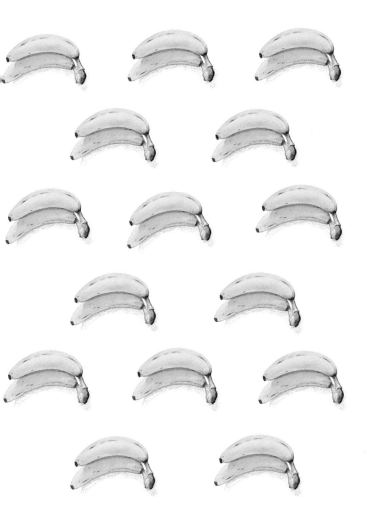